It started as an ordinary day. clock on the mantlepiece and was doing some embroidery when a maid came into the drawing room and said there were three gentlemen at the door wishing to speak with her on a matter of great urgency. Lady Frobisher seemed very surprised and I am sure she wasn't expecting anyone to call today. I was told to finish what I was doing and leave the room while she entertained her guests in private.

Three dark-suited men were shown in to see Lady Frobisher. I retreated next door and continued to do the dusting while listening to the door of the drawing room which was inadvertently left ajar. Lady Frobisher was a strict Mistress in her mid-forties, tall and slim. She had an elegance about her which wasn't too surprising when one considers her breeding. No doubt she went to finishing school and learned the art of deportment at a very early age, which

had paid off handsomely as she oozed sophistication.

Now, being a woman I couldn't say for sure, but I think most men would find Lady Frobisher quite attractive as she was slim, well-educated and seemed very sexual. However, apart from her maids who included me, she lived alone as her husband was away a lot on business trips that lasted weeks and months sometimes. To my mind, it was a marriage that lacked any passion at all.

The three men looked very solemn as they entered Lady Frobisher's drawing room. Visitors were such an unusual advent I decided to eavesdrop as much as I could, made easier with the drawing room doors left slightly ajar and I could hear everything that was said.

"Please take a seat," Lady Frobisher said to her guests suggesting a sofa opposite hers. Madam waited until they took off their hats and seated themselves comfortably.

"What brings you, gentlemen, here today?" Lady Frobisher asked sensing that something was very wrong with the men's bearing and attitude.

"The man in the middle who was taller and older than the others took the role of spokesman and said:

"Unfortunately we are the bearers of bad news Lady Frobisher," the man said apologetically. "I am sorry to inform you, your husband was killed in a road accident in Istanbul last Wednesday." Lady Frobisher seemed stunned by the announcement, so much so one of the men called me into the room and requested a glass of water for the lady. I immediately went to the pitcher and poured my lady a glass of water and took it to her. The poor woman seemed very pale and ashen, she was clearly very upset with the news. When Lady Frobisher finally composed herself and asked in a faltering voice:

"Why has it taken three of you to bring me this dreadful news?" she asked.

"My name is Wilfred Drummer, of Drummer and Drummer Solicitors, Oxford Oxon. These are my colleagues Brian Drummer and Colin Drummer, he said, pointing to the two men on either side of him.

"Are you here to tell me the contents of my husband's will?" Lady Frobisher asked. "My husband has always told me he will leave me well provided for in the advent of his untimely death."

"Yes, that does bring us to the matter in hand," replied Wilfred Drummer in a very composed and professional way. "I am afraid to say I am the unfortunate bearer of further bad news, to that I have already told you. Your husband was deeply in debt and because of this there is only a small pension, just enough for your daily needs."

"Well, that's something I suppose," Lady Frobisher replied, trying to take all this dreadful news in, in one sitting, "at least I shall inherit the house, won't I?."

"I'm afraid not," Colin Drummer said, speaking for the first time. "Frobisher Hall has several mortgages against it and will have to be sold in the shortest time possible to satisfy the creditors."

Lady Frobisher came over quite dizzy and I was sent off to find an extra shawl for her to wear as she appeared to be shivering from the cold. I assumed she was in deep shock, her world was instantly rocked by the presence of these three strangers.

"What am I to do, where am I to go?" She asked in desperation.

"Your late husband left Frobisher Hall to you and the remaining assets to Alice Frobisher. I assume he thought your sister would look after you, but that is, by the by, because your sister is deceased so everything will by default become yours. According to our calculations once Frobisher Hall is sold," said Brian Drummer, "there will hopefully be enough funds left for you to downsize and buy something more modest leaving you with enough pension for your daily needs."

"I shall have to let my staff go," Lady Frobisher said as she grappled with the immensity of her problems.

"If our calculations are correct it may leave you with enough funds to retain one maid," said Brian in consolation.

'I have to inform you Frobisher Hall has been put up for auction a month from today," added Wilfred Drummer. "I suggest in the meantime, you have the house contents valued and put up for auction before the sale of the house. You will also need to give a month's notice to your staff as soon as you can. We can help you with all of the above, so there is no need to stress yourself, we will endeavour to make your transition as painless as possible. My staff will also find you a new home fitting your status and income. You may need to rent initially until all your late husband's debts have been paid."

With those remarks, the gentlemen stood to go to the door. Wilfred turned to Lady Frobisher and added:

"You don't need to worry about a thing we'll be in constant touch. All you need to decide in the meantime is which member of your staff you intend to retain and take with you when you leave the Hall."

I showed the men out of the house where they had a waiting carriage. I returned to Lady Frobisher, who was shaking from all the news and told me to go and make a pot of tea. When I returned with the tea she asked me to get all the house staff together in the reception hall for a meeting at 5 pm as she had something important to say. Of course, my lady was unaware that I had heard everything the gentlemen had said.

At 5 pm I managed to assemble all the staff which included the cook, two scullery maids, two maids-of-all-work which included me and one male maintenance cum garden worker. We stood in a semi-circle waiting for Lady

Frobisher to appear and address us. We were waiting, chatting away for a good ten minutes before Lady Frobisher appeared from the drawing room. She stood and looked at each of us silently for a moment or two. The room became silent as the staff sensed something bad was about to be imparted to them and all the chatter slowly stopped. Then, as the silence was becoming unbearable the Lady of the house spoke:

"Some of you have been loyal servants for years," she said, looking at the cook in particular. I had a visit today from some gentlemen who told me my husband had died in an accident and has left considerable debt. It is my sad duty to inform you Frobisher Hall must be sold to pay the bills." Lady Frobisher stopped speaking to access the reaction of her staff.

"What happens to us?" asked one of the scullery maids.

"I am afraid," Lady Frobisher said, fighting back tears. "I must let you all go. You will get a month's notice and all will receive excellent references." With that remark, Lady Frobisher asked if there were more questions and then dismissed us to go about our duties and Lady Frobisher retreated before she lost her composure.

Over the next few days, I saw a marked change in Lady Frobisher's attitude to her staff. I suppose it could be the stress of an enormous change in her personal circumstances or more likely the sale of Frobisher Hall, which had been in the family since the middle ages. Lady Frobisher had become more aggressive and less inclined to forgive any mistakes made by her servants.

I too became the focus of Lady Frobisher's wrath. Every Monday morning the local farmer's son would bring fresh vegetables and eggs to the Hall, he enjoyed teasing and flirting with me. We just fooled around light-hearted for a few minutes and he would be off until next Monday, his presence broke the monotony for me. But this particular Monday Tom the farmer's son had me pinned in a corner and managed to steal a kiss and squeeze my left breast. The whole episode only lasted a second or two, but when he released his embrace who could I see out of the corner of my eye, but Lady Frobisher who gave me a look that could kill? She didn't say anything at the time, but I was summoned to the drawing room later in the day.

"You wish to see me Lady Frobisher," I said, giving the woman a customary curtsey as I entered the drawing room.

"Yes, young lady I do wish to see you. Come and stand closer to me, I'm in no mood for shouting," she replied in her most scolding of voices. I stepped closer to my Mistress. "Stand to attention you slovenly little hussy when I talk to you." I stiffened up a bit as I waited for a diatribe of abuse.

"I don't need to tell you the rules do I, Alice," Lady Frobisher said eyeing me up and down. "Not only do I catch you kissing and condoling with the farmer's son, which is against the rules, but you do it in my time. What do you have to say for yourself, don't bother giving me lame excuses?"

"I am sorry Mistress," I said, giving an extra curtsey to try and impress. "It was Tom he had me pinned against a wall against my will. I couldn't stop him or break away."

'Do you usually laugh and giggle when you're about to be assaulted against your will?" Lady Frobisher said with scorn. "It just seems to me to be a peculiar way to brush off unwanted advances. I don't believe a word of it. It has happened before hasn't girl? I will not abide by bad behaviour in my house. Go and see Mary the cook and ask her to give you six of the birch. You may go," she said, shooing me off to the door.

I left Lady Frobisher and made my way to the kitchen. I felt it was an additional humiliation for me to ask the cook for my own punishment. It was about lunchtime when I arrived in the kitchen. Everyone was dashing about serving lunch to Lady Frobisher and her guests.

Mary said she would punish me after the servants had their lunch. I hadn't been sent to the cook for punishment before and didn't know what to expect. All of us servants sat down in the kitchen for lunch as normal. Mary said prayers on our behalf and after a lunch of cold meat and bread, we cleared the kitchen table away. At this point, I thought I had been forgotten about and started to relax until I saw the cook go over to the far end of the kitchen and take from a peg on the wall a birch. All the staff on seeing the birch hurriedly left the kitchen for their duties and the cook and I were left alone.

"Alice," the cook said in quite a matter-of-fact tone whilst whisking the birch. "Bend over the end of the kitchen table." To be told by the coo to bend over the table for a birching, was hideously humiliating, even more so when she lifted my skirt and pulled down my drawers. W were both servants, both Lady Frobisher employees, but I got no dispensation for our joint status. The birch was brought down on m buttocks with full force and I was in a heap of tears by the time I received all six strokes.

"Go and put the birch back on its page for me please," the cook said with no more emotion than if she had just stirred the broth. When I had straightened my dress and wiped my eyes, I put the birch back on its peg on the wall.

"I'll inform Lady Frobisher you have been dealt with satisfactorily." With those words, I was sent back to continue with my chores.

Chapter Two

The auctions

Frobisher Hall had never been so busy there were dozens of people coming and going. They were examining the lots of furniture, paintings and garden furniture set to be sold in the afternoon auction. Mable and I were given the job of carrying a tray of drinks for anyone who wanted one. During a lull in activity, Mable came over and stood beside me and said in a low voice.

"Have you had your redundancy letter and severance pay yet?

"No," I replied.

"I'm surprised," Mable said, "Everyone had their letter and pay given to them this morning personally by Lady Frobisher."

"Everyone," I asked, wanting clarification.

"Yes, all the staff, including the cook," Mable assured me.

"I wonder why I haven't received mine," I said becoming a bit concerned I had been forgotten about.

"Perhaps Lady Frobisher couldn't find you this morning. I expect you'll get your letter later," Mable said reassuringly.

The auction had now started and Mable and I were busy passing out drinks as the punters entered the bidding hall. By late afternoon Frobisher Hall didn't look the same anymore as most of its furnishings had been taken away by their new owners. I tried to find Lady Frobisher to find out about my severance pay, but she was nowhere to be found.

There were all sorts of gossip going on downstairs and some of the staff left with the furniture without serving out their notice. Mable was right everyone without exception had gotten a letter of redundancy except me. The next morning a coach arrived at the Hall steps and out stepped Lady Frobisher she had come to collect some personal belongings. Before leaving again I was called to the drawing room by my Mistress.

I felt a bit relieved as I thought she must have realised I had yet to be given a redundancy letter and notice to quit. So I assumed that was all she wanted to see me for and it was simply a matter of passing me an envelope and thanking me for my service and saying goodbye. When I arrived in the drawing room Lady Frobisher seemed as obnoxious as always, whereas I had expected her to be a bit conciliatory as I was leaving. I stepped into the room and gave my Mistress a customary curtsey, thinking it would be the last, and stepped close enough to be passed an envelope, except none was forthcoming.

"Ah, there you are Alice, come and sit down opposite me on the sofa. I have a fresh pot of tea, would you like a cup?" Mistress asked.

'I didn't know what to say, it is very unusual for a servant to be offered a cup of tea by her Mistress, if not completely unheard of. I was slow in replying so Lady Frobisher took on herself to pour me a cup anyway.

'I hardly need to tell you, Alice, Frobisher Hall has been sold to pay off my late husband's debts. You, me and the servants have to be out of here in two weeks for the new owners to take over the Hall. Unfortunately, the new owners will be coming with their own staff hence the redundancies.

Yes Mistress, that reminds me, you haven't as yet given me my redundancy letter," I said almost holding my hand out in anticipation.

Be patient Alice, I will come to the question of your redundancy in good time. Now may I continue please?" Lady Frobisher asked with a hint of annoyance in her voice.

"Yes, sorry Mistress," I replied like a scorned puppy with its tail between its legs.

"I should think so. I may not be the Lady of Frobisher Hall anymore, but I am still your Mistress and you'll continue to speak only when you're spoken to, do you understand?" she asked.

"Yes Madam, sorry Madam," I replied, annoyed that I am showing such deference when I am about to be sacked.

"I have completely lost my thread now, oh yes, remember. As you, no doubt noticed I have been absent these last few days. I have been house hunting in the local area. With the help of my accountants and solicitors Drummer and Drummer, I had enough funds from the sale of the Hall and artefacts left to buy a more humble dwelling."

Lady Frobisher stopped speaking to take a sip from her tea, and as she did so she eyed me up and down. She passed me a plate of biscuits and said.

"Go on," She said, "take one." I took a biscuit and bit into it and then Mistress continued.

"I have carefully worked out my expenses and I have just enough funds to take a maid with me to my new home. Would you like the position? I warn you I won't be able to pay you as much as you get here at the Hall, but I will be able to provide pocket money, food and board. What do you say?" She asked, insisting I take another biscuit. I was slow to reply and pretended to be chewing my biscuit to give me extra seconds to think. I was in two minds. I didn't like Lady Frobisher very much, but life is hard in the 1900th century and if I didn't secure a position very quickly I would soon find myself in the workhouse. As anyone who ever had the misfortune to end up in the workhouse will tell you, it is no place to go and was very much the very last resort.

So I didn't have a lot of choices, it was staying with a devil I know or going out into the cold, hard wide world and taking my chances. I decided to go with the devil. I was also curious why she chose me to be her maid when Mable would have been a better choice, Mable had never been sent to the cook for the birch, she was always obediently efficient and doesn't flirt with men, whereas I was the troublesome one.

"Well, I don't have all day Alice, you want the position or not?" Lady Frobisher asked waiting impatiently for my reply.

"Yes, please Madam," I said almost kicking myself for taking the easy way out and lacking the gumption to step into the unknown.

"Good, Good," repeated my Mistress. " A coach will pick you up in the morning and take you to our new home. It will need spring cleaning from top to bottom before I move in. You may go now and get on with your duties." I thanked Lady Frobisher and left her in the drawing room with her tea and biscuits.

Chapter Three

Weeping Willow Cottage

I was up early, packed and waiting by the Hall door for my coach to arrive. Dawn was breaking revealing a very foggy, cold grey day. I could hear a coach cutting through the gravel long before it came into sight. The black coach pulled up right outside the Hall's front doors and the driver shouted down without moving from his seat.

"Are you Miss Alice Simms?"

"Yes," I replied.

The driver climbed down from his seat and took my cases and tied them to the back of the carriage. "Hop aboard it is nice and warm inside we'll be on the road for around an hour and a half." He said climbing back on the driver's bench. I had the whole inside of the coach to myself. It was indeed warm and comfortable, although the suspension could have been better and by the time we arrived at our destination I had quite a sore bottom as it felt the brunt of every pothole and rock we travelled over. I was glad to have reached my destination.

I looked out of the window with great curiosity as the coach pulled into the village and made its way down a narrow tree-lined road until it reached the house. The house, although very small by Lady Frobisher's standards was still a very big house to the eyes of a mere mortal like myself. I suppose rather than a stately hall the true definition of this house was more a manor house. Although it had the curious name Weeping Willow Cottage. I guessed it might have as many as eight or so bedrooms. The house was Georgian in period and constructed in red local brick, at the front door, stood Lady Frobisher waiting to greet me on my arrival.

Here you are," Lady Frobisher said with an insincere smile. "I show you to the maid's quarters so you may quickly change into your uniform as there is much to be done. The whole house needs a spring clean from top to bottom." Lady Frobisher showed me my room and left me to change and to come and find her in the living room when I was ready.

When I ventured back downstairs, I found my Mistress between rooms. "Let's take a look at you, Alice," she said, casting an eye up and down my uniform, "Yes you'll do for now. I will show you the kitchen and you can make us both a pot of tea as I am sure you're parched from the journey."

I was left in the kitchen to brew the tea and when I returned to the living room with a tray o tea I was told to sit down with Mistress to drink my tea and sign some papers.

"Papers to sign," I repeated a little confused as had never before been asked to sign any documents. I was a little worried too, I wasn't educated and couldn't read very well and wasn' at all sure what I will be signing.

"Yes," Mistress said, passing me a sheet of paper and a pen. I picked up the sheet of paper and looked at it. It may as well have been written in Chinese as in English as I couldn't read it under either circumstance.

"I'm sorry Ma'am," I said apologetically. "I can't read very well, what does the document say?"

"Oh don't worry your pretty little head over that. You can sign your name I suppose?"

"Yes Mistress," I replied.

"Then sign my dear, I'll tell you what the document means later when we have more time." I could see Lady Frobisher was getting impatient and I didn't want to rile her anymore. I assumed the document wasn't of that much importance and was just an acknowledgement of my position as her maid. So reluctantly, I scribbled my name on the dotted line.

"Excellent," Lady Frobisher replied as she added her own signature.

"Do I have a copy?" I asked.

"Alice, what do you want a copy if you cannot read? Oh, very well, I get you a copy later," she said brushing the matter aside. "I shall be taking on a part-time cook and scullery maid, you'll be my only full-time servant."

"What will my pay be?" I asked. "Do I get a day off a week as before?"

"Your pay will be threepence a week and one afternoon off a month but you're not to leave the house."

"That's a quarter of what I earned before and I had one day off a week," I argued.

"That's the terms you just signed up to. The contract lasts for five years and at the end of that period, we can discuss your payment again. If you have given me loyal service during that period I may increase your wage to sixpence a week.

"That will still be half of what I had last week," I said in disgust.

"Well, young lady that is what you have just signed for. I hope you're not going to bleat for the next five years that would be most tiring. When you have drunk your tea you may make a start by brushing the landing rugs."

Later that afternoon Mistress gave me an alarm clock and told me my day starts at 6 am to 9 pm with two ten-minute tea breaks and half an hour for lunch and dinner. I hadn't been here a whole day and was already regretting my decision to come to Weeping Willow Cottage.

Mind you it was a cold winter with snow and frost on the ground. At least I had hot food and a roof over my head. I decided to count my blessings, but the work was hard and the drudgery monotonous. The only thing that kept me sane was the friendship I sparked with the part-time cook and the scullery maid, they were both young girls about my own age.

Below stairs, we were in a world of our own. We would laugh and joke as we peeled vegetables for Madam's lunch and dinner. The cook would often sit and chat as she plucked a goose or a chicken. I felt sorry for the scullery maid who would be left with cleaning up the mess afterwards, which would be spread across the kitchen floor. This was our space as Mistress would rarely if ever come into the kitchen, so we felt free to frolic like children down here without Lady Frobisher's wrath.

One afternoon I was chasing the scullery maid around the kitchen table. I had taken her vegetable knife and she wanted it back, so ran around and around the huge oak kitchen table

rying to escape each other. It was a silly game,
but these infantile frivolities helped pass the
time. Then when we were getting puffed out
chasing each other around in circles Lady
Frobisher came to the kitchen door. This was
almost unheard of and both I and the maid were
stunned to see her there. Lady Frobisher looked
and sounded annoyed with us and said curtly:

Alice, I want to see you in my study before you
have your lunch." With those words, Mistress
had gone without admonishing us for fooling
around. I just assumed I will be told off when I
see her in the study later.

Chapter Four

Promotion

I knocked on the study door and entered when I heard Lady Frobisher beckon me in. Madam was sitting doing some embroidery and she put down her needlework to talk to me.

"Come and sit next to me," she said patting the seat. "I have been studying the accounts and I have a little more cash than I expected at the end of the month."

"Does that mean I can have a pay rise, Madam?" I asked excitedly.

"No, it doesn't," Mistress replied without any hesitation. You don't deserve a pay rise. What it does mean is I can afford Mable the scullery full time she'll become a maid-of-all-work and you my dear will become my lady's maid.

So straight after lunch, I want you to report to my bedroom. Now when you return to the kitchen please send Mable up to see me,"

Madam said dismissing me. I gave a quick bob and left the room.

I had my lunch below stairs as it is referred but in actual fact was the kitchen which is considered a servants' area a place where the Mistress will rarely go. So now there were two full-time servants and a part-time cook. I got on with the staff really well and was a happy bunny especially now Mable was moving into the house. However, I realised now I have been promoted, as Madam describes the position, to Lady's maid I won't be seeing so much of the other staff in future. To my mind, it was barely a promotion as my wages remain as they were before.

After lunch, I reported to Lady Frobisher's bedroom as requested. I knocked and entered and gave the usual curtsey as I stepped into the room.

"Ah, here you are Alice, come and brush my hair we need a chat about your new responsibilities and duties," Mistress said passing me a hairbrush. "Be gentle," she added don't tug on the knots, tease them out instead." I began brushing away at my Lady's shoulder-length grey hair. "Um, that's nice there is something therapeutic about having one's hair brushed. I could fall asleep," Madam said as she enjoyed the experience.

I brushed away for about five to ten minutes before my Mistress spoke again, my hair brushing seemed to send her off into a trance.

"Now to discuss your duties as a Lady's maid," Mistress said breaking the silence. A lady's maid's specific duties included helping me with my appearance, including make-up, hairdressing, clothing, jewellery, and shoes. You will also remove stains from clothing; sew.

mend, and alter garments as needed; bring my breakfast into my bedroom. You will draw my bath. However, you will not be expected to dust and clean every small item as that would be the job of a Mable the housemaid. Do you understand your broad duties?" Lady Frobisher asked.

"Yes," I replied, continuing to brush Mistress's hair.

"Good," Mistress replied, "so you'll understand from now on you'll be spending much more time up here in my bedroom than elsewhere in the house. "You may start by running me a bath. Don't forget to use your elbow to check the temperature of the water, if it is too hot you'll be in trouble."

I put down the hairbrush and went next door to the bathroom and began running the water. I don't know how many times I dipped my elbow in the water to ensure it wasn't too hot, I didn't fancy the wrath of my Mistress on my first morning as a lady's maid. Before I finished running the water Mistress stepped into the bathroom completely naked, I was quite startled as I wasn't expecting her to stand before me starkers. I expected her at least to wear a towel or a dressing gown to save her blushes and mine.

"Don't look so startled," Lady Frobisher said, amused at my naivety. "You didn't expect me to get into the bath dressed, did you? Come on step out of the way and let me get into the bath." I waited until Mistress was in the bath and I turned to go back into the bedroom.

"Where are you going?" asked my Mistress.

"I thought you were finished with me," I replied, turning back into the room.

'I'm not bathing myself, come here and scrub my back," she said passing me the loofah. I scrubbed her back, I had never bathed anyone before and felt very self-conscience and awkward with my new task. When I had finished Mistress passed me a flannel. "Now soap up the flannel and wash my breasts. Come on girl they don't bite, you have seen breasts before, you have breasts don't you?"

I began to gingerly wash Madam's voluptuous breasts. I confess I did feel titillated as wiped the flannel around her wholesome breasts. I mentally chastised myself for such stirrings, after all, I am a woman and should be attracted to my own sex, should I?

"Now you may wash my private parts," Mistress said, spreading her legs for me. I rubbed the flannel down between her legs and when I finished Lady Frobisher suddenly stood up giving me an impromptu shower. Mistress put a wet hand on my breast and squeezed the nipple.

"Are you becoming aroused petal?" She asked sarcastically.

Madam stepped out of the tub and I immediately began to dry my Mistress. My Mistress had a fine trim body for a lady in her late forties. She knew it too, and she sensed I was excited by seeing her in her state of undress and revelled in it.

"You may stay and clean and tidy the bathroom," Madam said as she retired back to the bedroom. I spent about twenty minutes cleaning up the bathroom before returning to the bedroom where Mistress lay naked on top of the bed covers. When she saw me she sat up.

"Come here, Alice," she commanded. "Would you like to suck my breasts?" I was taken aback by this suggestion and faltered. "Come sit on the edge of the bed," she said, patting where I was expected to sit. "It's okay," she said crooning. "You have a nice suck and enjoy."

I hadn't imagined I would enjoy sucking another woman's breasts, but I took to it like a duck to water and was becoming more titillated and aroused as I sucked. Suddenly she stopped me sucking and began to get up.

"That's enough for today young lady, now you can help me dress," Mistress said going towards the wardrobe. She picked a black dress which I had to help her climb into and button up at the rear.

"You have some lovely dresses, Madam," I said admiring her wardrobe.

"Later, when we have got to know each other better, I may let you wear one of my dresses, would you like that?"

"Yes Madam," I replied.

Madam retired to the lounge and I was told to remain in her bedroom and clean, tidy and come to find her when I had finished. When I had finished cleaning the bedroom I went downstairs to find Lady Frobisher. I found her in the living room doing her embroidery. Mable was flapping about doing some dusting when Mistress told her to leave the room, leaving us two.

"Come here, Alice," Mistress demanded. I stepped forward and gave a customary curtsey. "Now kneel here in front of me."

"Kneel," I questioned indignantly.

"Yes kneel, are you too good to kneel in front of your Mistress?" I was very reluctant to do so. "Kneel," Mistress repeated, raising her voice. I had little choice but to do as she asked and I slowly dropped to my knees. When I was on my knees, I found being forced to submit to my

Mistress strangely titillating, and this caused me to grapple with my thoughts, why should I be feeling this way?

"That's better," Mistress said approvingly. "You need to know your place young lady, things will be a bit different from now on. From time to time I may need to chastise you, do you know what I mean by the word chastise?" Madam asked me. It wasn't a word I was familiar with so I replied.

'No Madam."

'Remember at the Hall when I sent you to the cook for the birch that is chastisement."

'Oh," I replied inadequately not liking the sound of what she was about to say.

'The difference being in the future, I shall chastise you myself personally." I was about to protest, but Lady Frobisher went on to say I was now indentured to her for five years and if I was to leave her employ in that time, she would make sure I never worked again in service.

"Any questions," barked my Mistress as she peered down at me on my knees as if I was something the cat had dragged in.

"Yes Madam, when do I get paid I have been here a month now and you haven't paid me a thing," I asked cowering a bit as I feared the answer.

"Pay, pay," you ask. What do you want money for? You're provided with food and warm lodgings aren't you, you ungrateful girl?"

"Yes Madam," feeling foolish for having the audacity to ask for an agreed wage.

"What are you going to spend money on; you only have one afternoon off a month, if I let you have that much time off. No, you're quite alrigh as you are. If it wasn't for me and my generosity you'll be in the poor house now."

"Back to the matter in hand, pay indeed," she scoffed as an afterthought. "I expect and demand total and absolute obedience from you from now on, anything less and you'll be punished severely. I own you now you're mine until the end of your indentures. Now you can go into the kitchen and help the cook prepare dinner. You'll bring me breakfast in bed at 7 am sharp."

That was the last I saw of my Mistress until the next morning when I brought a tray of breakfast to her room.

"Have you had breakfast, Alice?" she asked me.

"Yes Madam," I replied with a shallow bob.

"Then you may kneel here at the side of my bed." I did as I was told and went down on my knees.

"Put your knees together and hands in your lap, eyes cast down," Mistress demanded. I did as requested. "That's better a nice submissive pose for your lady," Lady Frobisher said approvingly. In future whenever I ask you to kneel to me this is the position you'll adopt."

When Madam finished her breakfast I was told to take the tray away to the kitchen and return and run the bath. When I returned Mistress was asleep, but I ran the bath and when it was ready I returned to the bedroom to find Mistress was still slumbering. I shook Lady Frobisher's shoulder to be met with a barrage of abuse.

"What are you doing servant girl? What is the meaning of shaking me?"

"You were asleep and your bath is ready," I replied shocked by her reaction.

"Listen carefully Alice, the way to wake your Mistress is to shake my pillow only until I arouse."

I bathed Madam in the same manner as the morning before, except this time she wanted me to rub her nipples with a soapy cloth until they became erect. Madam lay there in the bath and softly groaned and then in the bath water she played with herself until she became orgasmic. I just stood there and watched her pleasure herself.

After the bath, I helped Lady Frobisher dress and then she sat at the dressing table and told me to put her makeup on. I felt really strange putting someone else makeup on, I wasn't that good at doing my own makeup. However, Mistress seemed satisfied with my efforts and when she put on her perfume she gave me a squirt. Her perfume was too musty for my liking, I preferred a more fruity fragrance, but I appreciated the small gesture.

I spent the remainder of the afternoon cleaning her boudoir and tiding away her clothes. Madam had become deliberately untidy and clothes were just strewn everywhere. Everything was left for me to fold up and put away neatly in the drawers and wardrobe.

When Madam's room was thoroughly cleaned I was to report to the kitchen and help prepare dinner. There was a knock at the kitchen door and as everyone was busy I went to answer it. To my surprise, it was the farmer's son Tom, who had brought a basket of free-range eggs. It was the first time I had seen him since he delivered at Frobisher Hall.

I was excited about seeing him so was everybody else in the kitchen, we all loved Tom as he was always cheerful and friendly. Mable and the cook both knew he had a soft spot for me, so they turned a blind eye when we flirted with each other. Tom took advantage of the situation and dragged me laughing into the pantry and shut the door. Alone we kissed and hugged, then he dropped his trousers spun me around and bent me over the panty table and pulled up my skirt and lowered my panties.

He was just about to do the deed when whom should see open the pantry door but Lady Frobisher. Tom quickly pulled up his trousers in a flash, but the damage was done, it was clear what was about to take place.

'You may leave Tom. You not to return to the cottage and I will be telling your father we will not be requiring your services again.

"We were just flirting," Tom said unconvincingly. Lady Frobisher was not interested in his pleas and pointed him to the kitchen door. She saw him as no more than an uncouth labourer of the lowest order.

"Go," she bellowed. "And you Alice go straight to the drawing room and wait for me."

I knew she was in no mood to be messed with, so I straighten my dress and left for the drawing room. I waited in the drawing room for ages for my Mistress to arrive. I dared not sit as I thought that would look disrespectful and put me into deeper trouble, so I paced up and down the room until my Mistress arrived. Finally, Lady Frobisher entered the room and in her right hand, she held a white leather riding crop, which she used to tap the palm of her left hand as she spoke.

'On your knees," she barked. I went straight down on my knees and I assumed the position I was taught earlier. "I know what you and Tom were up to. I thought I had nipped this tomfoolery in the bud back at Frobisher Hall. It would seem the birch had not deterred you from gross misbehaviour. I may seem like a spoilsport, but I, in the nick of time, saved you from a fate far worse than me catching you out. Where do you think babies come from Alice?" Madam asked. The question surprised me and seemed a bit beside the point. "To help you it has nothing to do with storks."

From having sex," I replied.

Correct and what were you about to do?" Lady Frobisher asked, but before I could reply she answered for me. "You were about to have unprotected sex with Tom. Now let me ask you another question, Alice. What do you think will happen if you fall pregnant?" I was a bit lost for an answer.

"Come on Alice answer, okay I will tell you. I won't be able to keep you on, you'll be no use to me nursing a newborn baby. You'll be discharged from my services and put on the street. You'll have nowhere to go except to the workhouse. I probably do not need to tell you what the workhouse staff think about feckless single mothers. I have saved you from a fate far far worse than death." Mistress stopped talking for a moment to catch her breath, she continued to tap the riding crop on her palm which prompted me to ask.

"Are you going to ride today, Madam?"

"Oh the crop," Lady Frobisher remarked, looking down at the implement, no this is for you. You need to be punished severely. Right, where shall we have you, come here and bend over the back of the sofa." I did as I was told. Madam slowly lifted my skirt and folded it on my back out of the way. Then she slowly pulled down my knickers until they were just below my buttocks. At this point, I expected to feel the pain of the crop, but instead, Madam caressed my bottom for several moments before the punishment began. It would have been pleasant except I knew what was coming after.

Eventually, the crop descended onto my bottom, it was like being electrocuted, the pain was immense and between each stroke, I was lectured by Madam about morality and unwanted babies.

"I have decided to be much stricter with you for your own good. I have decided to cancel your monthly afternoon off, you cannot be trusted."

I began to remonstrate, but as I did so I was interrupted by the pain of another stroke of the riding crop.

"I shall give you more wholesome duties to keep your mind occupied and to take your mind off men. If you can fantasise about men you have too much time on your hands. If you are exhausted from a day's chores, you won't have energy enough to want to be in the pantry with strange men. Do you understand?"

"Yes Madam," I replied as the crop came down again, my sore, aching, stinging buttocks.

"Your day will now start at 5 am. You can do Mable's job and set all the fireplaces and empty the ash in the garden. When it is light you can draw all the house curtains back and then bring me my breakfast for 7 am. The new regime should keep you out of trouble."

Chapter Five

Drudgery

I had to get up earlier than 5 am to have time to wash, dress and makeup before my duties begin. I hardly felt as if I had any sleep at all. Getting up in the dark long before Madam or even the other servants was no fun at all. The house was deadly quiet as I set about my chores. My first job was setting the fireplaces. I had to shovel out all the ash and take it down to the bottom of the garden. It wasn't only dark, but the mornings were frosty too. When I returned from freezing outside I had to put down fresh newspaper, coal and kindling for the day. I had six fireplaces to attend to and when I have done this I had to wash off all the coal dust from my hands and arms before opening all the curtains and blinds as it became light outside.

By the time I heard the first bird tweet its morning song, I was already exhausted and in need of rest. I felt like I had already done a full day's work. However, the day had hardly begun. At 7 am, I took Madam her breakfast. As usual, I had to kneel at the side of her bed as she ate and read a magazine at the same time. I envied her between those nice warm sheets and blankets.

Between mouthfuls of food and hardly taking her eyes from her magazine, she said without any change in her voice.

"You may take your clothes off."

"My clothes off?" I questioned.

"Do you always have to repeat me? Yes, all of your clothes and then go back on your knees," Reluctantly, I did as requested and stripped off and put my folded clothes neatly on a nearby chair and then went back down on my knees again.

"Do you know why I have asked you to strip off Alice," Madam asked, turning away from her magazine to look at me.

"No Madam," I replied.

I want to impress upon you, you're no longer my servant, but instead you're now my slave. You'll need to understand I now own you, all of you, your mind body and soul. You are my slave for life. Do you understand?"

"No, not really," I replied.

Then, don't you worry your pretty little head, you soon will understand? Now go and stand at the end of the bed. Mistress puts the empty tray of food aside and climbed out of bed and stepped over to me. She ran her warm hands down my body and over my tits over and over again. She crooned and I felt her warm breath on my neck.

"I want to get to know every inch of my property," Madam said as she stroked my vagina and entered a finger or two. "Are you getting wet Alice," she asked mockingly. "Do I turn you on as much as Tom the farmer's boy? Do I titillate you?" I didn't answer any of her questions as I didn't think she was expecting m to reply.

On and on she explored my body as if I was a shop manikin or one of her favourite dolls. Madam left me for a moment or two, to return with a pot of baby oil and began to rub it all over my body until it glistened.

"You're a handsome young lady," she said, pushing the hair out of my eyes. Kiss me," she demanded. I did as asked, but for reasons, I can't explain I found it quite repugnant. I didn' mind Lady Frobisher playing with my tits and vagina, but kissing felt more of an affront, simply I suppose because she was another woman. Then Madam began to fuck me with her fingers and to my disgust, I was becoming more and more aroused until I quivered in orgasm.

"Oh you are a disgusting little hussy," Madam replied. "Now go and run me my bath," Mistress said without acknowledging my orgasm. When I finished bathing, dressing and making up my Mistress. I, as usual, had to tidy her bedroom and after report to the kitchen. By this time it was 3 pm and I was almost too tired to stand. I would slip into the pantry not to have fun and frolics with farmer's boys, but to catch five minutes of sleep when no one was looking. Yet again Lady Frobisher caught me sitting on the floor of the pantry with my back to the wall fast asleep.

"What are you doing?" bellowed a voice that penetrated my slumber. I sprang to my feet tripping and stumbling from being half asleep. Go to the drawing room this instant," she screamed. I ran out of the kitchen and into the drawing room. Once again, I had to wait anxiously an age before Mistress appeared. I was relieved to see this time she hadn't a riding crop in her hand, but I nevertheless knew I was in for a hard time.

I was standing in the centre of the room and Lady Frobisher walked around me, examining me as if I was an exhibit.

"I am beginning to think you want to go to the workhouse, or why else would you behave so badly? Am I right?" She asked.

"No Madam," I replied.

"Then why do you test me so much?" Madam asked, stopping her circling to stand in front of me.

"I was just so tired; I had to close my eyes for a moment or two," I replied. I won't do it again."

"No you won't do it again, I shall see to that," Lady Frobisher replied. "So I am working you too hard. I can't have the servants thinking I am some kind of an Ogre. You clearly need a rest and you shall have a rest. Come with me," she said leading out of the drawing room door into the kitchen and out into the garden. We walked midway down the garden until we arrived at two small sheds.

Lady Frobisher opened one of the shed doors and beckoned me in with her hand. I stepped in and was about to turn and speak when the door shut and I heard the bolt pull across.

"I'll be back after you have had a good long rest," I heard Mistress's voice say as she walked away.

The shed was almost empty with a dirt floor. All there was in the shed was a newish metal bucket. It was only late afternoon and I was already cold, I sat on the dirt floor and shivered. There was little light, no windows, just what came under the door and that was rapidly disappearing as night time approached. I cried, this couldn't be any worse than the workhouse at least the workhouse would be warm if nothing else could be said for it.

There was nothing for me to do, but sleep, doze and shiver. The shed wasn't big enough for me to pace up and down properly. I had no pocket watch, so I had no idea of the time or how long had been there. Several hours seemed to have passed when I heard Mable's voice.

"Are you in there Alice?" I heard her whisper.

"Yes," I said, can you let me out?" I asked

"No," Mable said, "there's a padlock on the bolt. have a sandwich for you and a bottle of water. 'll pass it under the door. Don't let the Mistress now as I'll get the sack." Mable slid the oodies under the door.

What time is it?" I asked.

About 8 pm," Mable said. "I must go, if Mistress hasn't let you out my morning I'll ring you something for breakfast." Then, without another word Mable had gone and I was ack on my own. My only company was the odd eow of a cat and a distant owl in the fields ehind the house. It was a very, very long night. didn't get a second of sleep, I was far too cold, Il I did was shiver and long for the morning at ast it will be a bit warmer when the sun comes).

At first light, Mable was sent with the keys to release me from the shed. She took me to the kitchen for a hot breakfast. Mable told me Mistress said I could have a bath and sleep until lunchtime and to attend her in the drawing room after lunch. I needed a bath after around twenty hours of nonstop shivering. It wasn't until I was enveloped in hot water did I begin to feel human again. I then when I finished bathing jumped into my bed, cuddled my teddy bear and fell asleep until lunchtime.

I dreaded seeing Mistress after lunch as I was expecting to be scolded again for my misdemeanours. I wasn't to be disappointed.

"Ah, here you are, come here and kneel at my feet," Lady Frobisher insisted. "Did you enjoy your afternoon and evening off?" she added.

"No Madam," I replied.

"It was to teach you a lesson. It wasn't so much about you falling to sleep on duty, but a lesson in reminding you who and what you are."

"What am I?" I asked.

"You're not my servant, you're not salaried staff, and you're the lowest of the lowest my slave and my property. The sooner you realise who and what you are, the better for you my girl.

"I am not your slave," I insisted an indignant tone to my voice.

"Oh yes, you are. You're indentured to me for the next five years with an option to renew. If you leave, you'll never work again and will spend the rest of your days in the workhouse. Let me explain something to you," Madam said, pointing to a chair behind me. I turned to look. 'See the cat sleeping there she has more rights than you do, you have no rights, not a single one. You are the lowest of all creatures, the dregs, get used to it."

"If you hate me so much, why did you invite me here to Weeping Willow Cottage, why not let me go with the rest of the staff at Frobisher Hall? I don't understand," I added.

"You're my slave that is all you need to know for now. Due to your impromptu holiday, my bedroom and bathroom are in a state, go and clean them now and wait upstairs until I arrive to check your work."

Chapter Six

Lady Frobisher's Secret

I left the drawing room and went directly to Madam's bedroom which looked like a tornado had passed through it, with clothes spread throughout the room, on the bed, floor, and over chairs. I had to deduce which need folding and putting away and which clothes needed to be taken downstairs to be washed. It took me an age just to tidy the clothes away before I began to clean. When I finished, I sat on the edge of Madam's bed and awaited her arrival. I suppose I had been sitting there around an hour when I heard Madam coming up the stairs. I immediately stood up as she came through the door. She pretty much ignored me and walked around the bedroom and bathroom checking my work. Then she puffed up some pillows and laid on the bed, fully clothed and studied me with her eyes whilst sporting a grin.

"Tell me Alice what is the first rule a slave should learn?" She asked.

"As I am not a slave, how should I know?" I replied indignantly.

"Then I'll demonstrate. Take your clothes off, all of them," Madam barked. I reluctantly did so. I should have just walked out of the room, but Lady Frobisher was right, I would be walking straight to the workhouse probably for the rest of my life, so I obediently stripped.

"Now, Lady Frobisher said, waiting for me to remove the last vestige of clothing. "See those pink dumbbells on the dressing table."

"Yes, Madam," I replied, turning to see them.

"Go and pick them up. Hold one in each hand and return to the end of my bed," she ordered. When I had done as requested she added. "Now hold out your arms as high as they will go and stay in that position until I tell you to move." I held the dumbbells out which seemed fairly light, to begin with, but it wasn't long before my arms began to strain.

"You're slipping hold the dumbbells up as I commanded. Come on, come on arms up." I used every ounce of energy to pull my aching arms up again.

"The first rule a slave should learn is total, absolute unwavering obedience. This is a lesson in obedience. You may lower the dumbbells and come and kneel at the side of my bed." I came and knelt down facing my Mistress as she lay on the bed. As taught I lowered my gaze, but Lady Frobisher put her hand under my chin and lifted my face up until our eyes met.

"You asked me a question earlier you wanted to know why I had taken you as my slave, rather than someone else, or why I didn't let you go with the rest of the staff of the Great Hall. Well, I will tell you," Madam said, pausing to gauge my reaction.

"Yes, please do Madam, I want to know why you have singled me out. I was no better or worse than any of the other staff."

"Well, Alice, I don't know about that, you're the only member of staff I caught frolicking with men. But that is not why I have made you my lifelong slave.

"Then why have you picked me?" I asked dying to know why I have been singled out for such treatment.

"How long have you been in my employ?" she asked

"Since I was 12 years old," I replied.

"And before you were 12 years old where were you then?"

"I lived at the Frobisher Hall with my mother who was also a maid," I replied

"Your stepmother," Lady Frobisher said, correcting me.

"My stepmother, but you're mistaken," I pleaded.

"No, your birth mother was my sister," Mistress said waiting for me to ask more.

"I don't understand, you're telling me we're related?"

"Yes, I can assure you I am telling you the truth. You are the illegitimate child of my sister born out of wedlock." Madam said.

"Your father was a servant, which explains why you couldn't be taken into the family fold and kept as a maid to hide the disgrace. Last year my sister died and she made me promise I would ensure you're provided for and will never end up in the workhouse. So as a parting promise and pledge to my sister's memory, I have kept my word, so far, hence bringing you with me to Weeping Willow Cottage.

"I don't suppose she intended me to be your slave," I added.

"That is bye the bye, here you are, my slave and that is what you shall be for the remainder of your life, so you had better get used to it my dear," Mistress said. Mistress moved over and tapped the bed.

"Come onto the bed and join me," she said. I clambered onto the bed and lay down beside my Mistress. "That's better, being my slave isn't all bad," she said as she fondled my right breast. My Madam took particular attention to stroking my nipple until it became erect, and then most unexpectedly, she twisted my nipple making me tense with pain.

"You'll learn to take pleasure in the pain I give you," she said, releasing her clamp-like grip on my nipple. My breast began to throb as she caressed it better. Then she leaned towards me and sucked my sore tit.

"We will be doing this a lot, now you may dress and go and help cook and prepare dinner," Mistress said turning over and facing away from me. I got up, dressed and went downstairs. Mable greeted me at the kitchen door.

"I think it is awful the way, Madam has been treating you," Mable said as she diced some carrots. "If she treated me like that I would leave straight away," she added putting the sliced carrots into a big stainless pot.

"It's okay for you Mable you have family in the village to look after you until you found new employment, but me, well, I have nowhere to go, no one to help me, I will be at the mercy of the workhouse."

"Well, it just doesn't seem right," Mable said, dismissing the topic for more mundane gossip.

Madam came down to the dining room and Mable and I served her dinner. She sat alone at the big table as Mable and I attended to her every need. Mable brought in her dessert and I poured another glass of red wine.

"You may go now Mable," she said. Mable retreated with a curtsey and left the room. I was about to do the same when Madam indicated she wanted me to stay. "You remain here I haven't finished with you yet Alice. Over in the corner of the room, you'll some boxes in them you'll see a Christmas tree and decorations you can start putting them up in the corner."

Well, there were worse things to do in an afternoon it was a better chore than scrubbing floors, so I set to work. I quite enjoyed myself as I had an artistic flair. I had been busy for an hour and Mable was sent to join me to finish the project. Later Lady Frobisher came into the dining room to see our work. Madam was carrying some parcels as she looked admiringly at the tree.

You have both done a good job," she said, passing the parcels to Mable. "Here are a couple of small presents for you and the cook you can open them in the kitchen. Mable thanked Madam profusely, curtsied several times and left for the kitchen, leaving just me and Lady Frobisher. Lady Frobisher had one tiny remaining box in her hand, but rather than passing it to me she opened it and put it down for the cat. The cat devoured the tiny box of cat eats in a second.

Don't look so sad Alice, there are no presents for you, presents are for employees and pets, and you're a slave, not an employee nor a valued pet, Christmas isn't for slaves. Now go to my bedroom and clean it, stay there until I arrive."

I realised it was a staged show by Lady Frobisher to humiliate and degrade me and it worked. I felt as if it was intended to make me feel, totally worthless and unloved.

Chapter Seven

Where has everyone gone?

I was determined to make the best of Christma with or without Lady Frobisher's blessings. Both Mable and the cook felt sorry for me and the way I had been treated and they did their best to make it up. Together in the kitchen awa from Lady Frobisher, we had a wonderful Christmas. The cook had squirrelled away extr eggs, flour and a plump chicken from the farm for us the servants to enjoy. We even managed to acquire a couple of bottles of red wine. In addition to the wine, the cook brewed some apple cider which had a kick like a mule.

It was almost unheard of for Mistress to require my services after seven in an evening and I thought it was safe to have a few drinks without the lady of the house ever knowing. Although banned from the house Tom the farmer's boy called by with some Christmas goodies. Indeed, all four of us get wildly drunk. This was a bit of a mistake as we got a bit animated and noisy and I thought at one stage I had heard someone approach the kitchen door. If it was Lady Frobisher she didn't come in, so I dismissed it as my imagination.

I wondered, considering it was the season of goodwill if she had heard us and come to the door, she chose to turn a blind eye and was going to overlook this small indiscretion. After all, it was Christmas and we were doing what millions of other people were doing, getting drunk and enjoying ourselves. We ate danced and sang until the early hours of the morning.

I had drunk far too much and overslept way past my get-up time. I woke up at 8 am hours after my official working day starts. I was already late with Lady Frobisher's breakfast. I dashed downstairs to prepare breakfast. The kitchen was empty, with no cook, and no Mable, I just assumed they had also overslept. I hurriedly assembled Madam's breakfast on a tray and dashed back upstairs to serve her in bed.

When I entered Lady Frobisher's room, she was already awake and sat up in bed reading a novel

"Oh, here you are," she said mockingly looking over the top of her book. "You don't look very well, are you ill my child," she added taking the tray from me. "You're very late with my breakfast, can you explain your slovenliness?"

"I am not going to lie," I answered, deciding to be truthful. "I had too much to drink last night."

"Yes, I know, I thought I heard a male voice too, did you by chance have any banned visitors?" She asked almost knowing the answer before I spoke.

'Yes," I said seeing no point in lying.

'Who was it," Lady Frobisher asked with great nterest. I was at this point I was tempted to lie ind make someone up, but I was hungover and n no mood or inclination to say anything other han the truth and damn the consequences.

'It was Tom the farmer's son," I replied with a oit of a frog in my voice.

"Tom," Lady Frobisher said loudly, "you don't mean Tom the farmer's lad who I had banned from this house just days before?"

"Yes Madam," I replied.

"Please don't take it out on Mable and the cook, it was my idea blame me. It was also my fault we all got drunk."

"Don't you worry your pretty little head I have already punished Mable and the cook," Mistress said biting into her breakfast.

"You have?" I asked.

"Yes, I have Alice, they have both been dismissed without references with immediate effect. They are probably both at the railway station at this minute waiting for the next train.'

"Who will now do their work?" I asked. "aren't you shooting yourself in the foot?"

'I have been thinking about that. I decided it was profligate having three members of staff when one will suffice. Yes, I mean you Alice, from now on you'll do all the domestic chores around the house every last one of them."

'Me," I replied.

Yes, you alone, but this isn't your punishment, I have yet to decide how I will punish you. I shall decide when I have finished my breakfast. Until then you may go and stand in the corner of the room like the naughty little girl you are. Go in, to the corner with you." I was incensed but went into the corner to calm myself down. I realised if I was dismissed, it wouldn't be the railway station for me, but a one-way ticket to the local poorhouse. Whatever punishment was coming my way I would have to endure it.

You may remove all your clothes," Madam's voice said from behind me. "Don't turn around, just strip your clothes off and leave them on the floor, you can pick them up later."I heard Madam put her tray down and come over and stood behind me. She ran her cold hands all ove my body taking extra interest in my breasts. She seemed to take extra pleasure from fondling my breasts.

"You have been a very naughty girl haven't you Alice," Mistress crooned, "and what happens to naughty girls to help them understand and mend their bad ways?" Madam asked.

"They are punished," I replied anticipating the reply required.

"That's right naughty girls must be punished severely or they will never learn to behave. It only begs the question of how should I punish you. Do you have any ideas, Alice?" I didn't reply it would seem potty for me to recommend my own punishment.

"What shall we do with you? You may stay here in the corner for a moment whilst I think." Lady Frobisher said, leaving the room. After a short while, she returned. I hadn't moved from the corner, I wondered if she had hoped to have found me sitting on the bed to have a further excuse to admonish me.

"To be fair with the dismissal of cook and Mable, you now have all the housework to do, your punishment could be said to be everlasting. To add to your drudgery your only company will be mine, for you another punishment in itself. However, I must mark your bad behaviour. Remember I once sent you to the cook for the birch. You seemed to enjoy that, so I am sending you into the garden to make me another one. You may go now and bring it to me in the drawing room when you have made it." I reached down for my clothes. "No Alice, you won't need those."

"But there is snow on the ground I'll freeze," I begged.

"Then you'll need to be quick, you'll find secateurs in the greenhouse. Off you go before I get angrier with you."

"May I at least wear my shoes?"

"No, you're under punishment, now go."

I knew further protests would get me nowhere. When I arrived at the back door, Mistress told me to wait. She came over to me dressed in her coat and gloves and put crocodile clamps on my breast nipples. Each clamp was connected to a long thin chain.

"I will show you where the secateurs and birch trees are," she said with a smirk. So we went outside into the garden together, me completely naked being pulled along by a chain. It was a good job we had no neighbours, it would have been a bizarre sight. In microseconds, I began to shiver wildly and my poor feet ached in the snow and ice. I was being pulled around to find a willow tree. Not only was I suffering from the cold, but my breasts were getting more sore by the second. I was eventually shown a tree and I was told to cut down twelve branches. When I had cut twelve branches, I was pulled back to the kitchen door and Madam released my nipple clamps. The pain of the clamps being removed made me double over in pain.

'You'll have to shred the leaves from the branches out here before you come in, it will make too much mess indoors," she left me outside and watched me through the kitchen door window pane strip all the leaves off each branch. When I had done, she opened the kitchen door for me to pass. Madam immediately passed me a roll of duct tape to bind the branches together and form a handle.

"Yes, you may go and stand by the wood burner to warm yourself while you add the finishing touches to your birch. Although I was grateful for the warmth from the burner, it hadn't stopped me from making uncontrollable shivers. Mistress pulled a chair out into the middle of the kitchen.

"This will take your mind off being cold," Madam said, taking the birch from me. "You have done a good job," she added admiring my handiwork. "Let's see how good it is, now bend over the back of the chair and grip the base hard." I was already suffering, but I could see there was going to be no mercy for me today.

In the kitchen window on the far side of the room, I could see a reflection of myself in the most humiliating position with my knickers and stockings pulled down. Worse still, I could also see a reflection of Lady Frobisher and saw she was relishing my discomfort and pain. She smiled with each stroke and it wasn't difficult to see she got sexual pleasure out of dominating me. When the punishment was over I was in tears which pleased my Mistress.

There, there," she said in mocking sympathy. If you were a good girl we wouldn't need to do these things. Now clear up all the bits of broken twigs and then you can go and cook dinner. You can cook, can't you Alice? Perhaps I should hold on to the birch for a day or two in case it is needed again."

don't know where Madam expected me to get my cooking skills from after all I was a domestic who has spent most of her life just cleaning. However, over the years I had watched the cooks prepare food so I had a bit of an idea. My first meal for Madam was chicken and rice in white sauce. Fortunately, I didn't need to make a sweet as there were already several prepared sweets in the pantry, which the cook had made before she was dismissed.

Madam seemed to be fairly pleased with my offering and after dinner, I tidied away the dishes.

"Would Madam like a sweet," I said with a dainty curtsey designed to impress.

"No, I don't think I shall, not this evening," Madam replied, taking my hand and giving it a bit of a stroke. "When you have eaten and tidie up come to my bedroom."

When I arrived in Madam's bedroom, she was already in bed despite only being about 7:30 pm.

"Here you are she said sleepily. Undress my dear and come on the bed," She said tapping the bedcover. I was very loath to obey I didn't war to be her sexual plaything, but once more I reminded myself what the poorhouse would be like, there would be no warm bed there beckoning me. I would be lucky to get a bail of straw to rest my weary body. I suppose I just had to get used to being what I am her slave and plaything. I reluctantly stripped off and climbed onto the bed. I was about to go under the covers when Madam said:

"No, wait," I want to see your bottom. "Oh," she said, rubbing her hands all over my buttocks, "Your bottom is so sore," she added coming out from under her covers. "Wait here," she said, getting up and going over to her wardrobe. She returned with four lengths of scarlet ribbon. She tied my hands together with the ribbon and then tied the ribbon to the bedpost. Then she did the same with my feet but spread-eagled and tied to each corner post.

"Now you're mine to have my evil way with," she said, climbing onto my tummy and caressing my boobs. "Your nipples are going nice and hard, you like this don't you, what a little hussy you are. You like being my little slave and captive." I didn't answer I didn't think it was worthy of an answer.

"You'll suffer a bit more pain for your mistress won't you Alice," she said tugging one of my nipples. "I'll show you something," she said, picking up a clear plastic bag from the dressing table. It was a bag full of clothes pegs but she had no intention of doing the laundry. Instead, she pinned about two dozen pegs on my breasts until hardly any flesh could be seen for wooden pegs. I groaned a bit as it was quite painful.

"What do you think I am going to do now?" Madam asked whilst kissing me. "What further delights do I have for you?"

"Please take them off," I begged, "the pegs are hurting me."

"Your wish is my command," Lady Frobisher said, getting off the bed and going back to the wardrobe. She returned with a riding crop and using just the leather flap at the end of the implement, she tapped each peg, one by one, until they snapped off my breasts. I was in agony as I wriggled and squirmed as each peg flipped into the air with the end of the riding crop. When all the pegs had been knocked off Madam said:

' That was fun. There, there," she said as she massaged each red and sore tit. "That will do for tonight," she added, releasing me from my bonds. "You may now climb under the covers and we will have a hug before we fall asleep.

After an extended fondle I fell asleep with my naked Mistress and that was where I remained until morning.

Chapter Eight

More Drudgery

I soon realised receiving the birch for the impromptu Christmas Party was only a minor part of my punishment, the real punishment was having been demoted once again to maid-of-all-work. I grafted from early morning to late at night. To add to my anguish Lady Frobisher checked all my work and one of her favourite pastimes was watching me scrub floors. Madam would often sit and just watch as I scrubbed the flagstones, gleefully pointing out the bits I had nissed. I think she was thrilled in seeing me on my knees obeying her every command.

One day whilst I was scrubbing the kitchen floor Mistress came over and stood in front of me. She had stepped into some of my suds and now was to clean and wipe her shoes. Whilst she stood there in front of me with her arms on her hips I went about wiping her shoes clean.

That's no good enough girl you have made them dirtier than they were, to begin with." She moaned.

My cloth is dirty from wiping the floor," I replied, looking up at the figure towering above me.

Then use your tongue," Mistress bellowed. I thought she was joking so I continued to wipe with the cloth.

"Didn't you hear me, your tongue girl use your tongue," Madam screamed down at me.

"No," I said. "I have had enough of you bullying me," I replied whilst bursting into an uncontrolled torrent of tears.

"We'll see about that," Lady Frobisher threatened, leaving me to finish wiping the floor. I watched her stomp out of the room and knew I was about to be in for a hard time, but even lowly maids can only take so much from their Mistresses. I felt elated that I had exerted and stood up for myself, but that soon turned to depression as I knew I was going to suffer all the more for my outburst.

I carried on with my duties waiting for Mistress to return and do something horrid to me, but I was left to get on with my chores unhindered. One of my duties was to polish and dust in the drawing room where I found Mistress doing h embroidery. Madam seemed to ignore me as I pottered around the room dusting then out of the blue she said:

It would seem," Madam said, breaking the silence, "that birching you or locking you in a shed overnight haven't tamed your spirit." I continued to dust and didn't respond to her remarks. "What do you think I need to do to break you in since I shall you know? You will become my loyal, obedient slave whether you like it or not. I will break you in, you mark my words," she said, putting down her handiwork and stepping over to me. Madam held up my chin with her hand and said:

'You're a defiant little hussy aren't you? Well, enjoy your little tantrum as it will be your last." Then Madam left the room for me to continue cleaning. After dinner that night I was ordered into the living room and told to strip off my clothes. When I had removed everything she then said. "On your knees," I went down on my knees and bowed my head submissively. "I have something for you. I have been saving it for a while now hoping I wouldn't need it, but you need a constant reminder of your status," she added.

Then she placed a cold shiny metal collar around my neck. With an Allen key, she locked the device so it can't be removed. It felt strangely heavy and uncomfortable.

"Go to your room and put your nightgown on and return here," Lady Frobisher said, "I will have another surprise waiting for you when you return." I left Madam and went to my room and put on my nightgown and returned to Mistress who was waiting in the drawing room. In her hand, she had a long metal linked chain which she padlocked one end to my collar. Then, without a word, she dragged me unceremoniously to the scullery. The free end of the chain she padlocked to a pipe under the sink.

"You can sleep here the night and every night until you can prove to me you have changed your ways." Well, it was better than the shed, but almost as cold, the big difference is I will have to sleep here every night.

"Can I have a blanket and pillow?" I asked as Mistress was leaving.

'The answer is no, you'll have to earn the privilege of a blanket or a pillow with good behaviour. Then in a month, we will see if you're ready to be allowed to go back to your room to sleep. I can tell you now, you'll appreciate your bed when you see it next. In the meantime," she said you may think of me asleep in my nice warm bed thinking of you here on the cold stone floor learning your lesson. You would have been in my bed tonight had you been good, instead enjoy." With those words, she left me to wallow in my misfortune and left me on the cold scullery floor.

In the morning after near sleepless night, I was awakened by a hard kick to my ankles. I looked up through sleepy eyes to see Lady Frobisher looking at me as if I was a mouse that had crawled out from under the skirting board.

"Slept well have we, "she said, watching me shiver from the cold," time to start work that will soon warm you up. You may dress and prepare my breakfast and serve it to me in the dining room," she added unlocking my chains but leaving my collar on. I pulled my aching body to my feet and went to my room and got dressed. Before I left to go downstairs, I looked at my lovely soft war bed and fantasised about sleeping for nine, or ten hours, but it was not to be.

went back downstairs and prepared Madam's breakfast and served it to her in the dining room as requested.

When you have had your breakfast you can change the linen on my bed and vacuum and clean the whole of the upstairs. As you're not using your bed there is no need to change your own linen, beds are for obedient, well-behaved slaves who do as they're told at all times."

took me all morning to clean the upstairs and in the afternoon I had lighter duties brushing Madam's hair and helping her with her makeup as she was invited out for the evening by a friend who had sent a coach to collect her at 7 pm. Just before she was ready to leave, she called me into the kitchen and made me lie face down on the stone floor, hog-tied and gagged me.

"I can't trust leaving you on your own anymore I don't want you running away with the family silver, you can lie here until I get back. Enjoy the rest," she added as she left the house.

If I knew I was going to be tied up by Madam, would have asked to go to the toilet as I was busting long before my Mistress returned. The only thing that took the discomfort of wanting pee was the cramp that affected my calf and hand muscles. It was a long evening lying there in the dark and cold listening out for my Mistress's return. I longed for her to return and release me from my bonds.

Finally, I heard a coach pulls up outside the house and muffled voices. Eventually, Madam came into the kitchen and lit a candle. She peered down at me as if she was looking at a goldfish in a bowl.

"So you survived the night then?" she asked, knowing I was gagged and couldn't reply. She knelt down and removed my gag. "Aren't you going to ask what a lovely evening I have had," she asked mockingly.

"I need a pee desperately," I begged.

"First things first," ask me if I had a nice evening," Lady Frobisher demanded raising her voice a tad.

"Have you had a nice evening Madam?" I asked wriggling with cramps and the need for a toilet.

"Thanks for asking," Mistress replied, "Yes, I have had a super evening." I knew without Madam saying she had been drinking, I could smell it on her breath. She also seemed slightly animated and not her usual self. "The food was excellent and we danced and drank punch, perhaps too much punch. Oh, you poor love, are you cold and that stone floor, let me release your bonds."

I was untied and allowed to go directly to the lavatory that is when I could manage to stand up straight after five hours or so hog-tied. When I returned Lady Frobisher showed me a damp patch on the floor.

"You have peed yourself, you disgusting little wrench. Go bath and change your clothes, put on your nightdress and come up to my bedroom." With those words, Madam retired and waited for my arrival. When I came into the bedroom Madam was already in bed reading. She looked up from her book and said:

"I should beat you for peeing on the floor, but the bed is cold you may come in beside me and warm me and the bed up." When I got under the covers Madam insisted I hugged her around the waist to warm her up. When my Mistress was a bit warmer she put her hand up the hem of my night dress and squeezed and caressed my breasts.

"You may sleep here tonight, I don't want you falling ill, an ill slave would be a burden." Although I was learning to hate my Mistress the warmth of her body and the softness of the bedclothes had me asleep in no time. At six am reality set back in, a foot had kicked me right out of the bed whilst I was still in deep sleep. I knocked my head on the bedside table and hit the floor with a thud. Mistress seemed totally unconcerned that there was blood coming from my forehead and ordered me off to make her breakfast.

In the kitchen, I wiped away the blood and I had quick bite of food before returning to the bedroom with Madam's breakfast on a tray. When I passed Madam the tray I was told to kneel at the side of her bed.

"After breakfast," Lady Frobisher said with a mouthful of food, "I am going to give you some obedience training." I cringed at the thought was that going to entail would be nothing I would care to do, I knew that much. "Obedience training will teach you, my dear, to obey me without a moment's thought. Slowly I will turn you into the passive, docile little slave that I long to own."

I helped Madam have a bath, and dress and helped her put on her makeup. She then went to a cupboard and selected a riding crop. I noticed she had several. Madam tried one or two by bending and flicking each crop until she finally settled on one, and then we both retired to the drawing room. When we entered the room, I was told to undress and put my folded clothes on the sofa. Then I was told to go down on all fours like a puppy dog. Madam got a pack of playing cards from a drawer and flicked them round the room. When all fifty-two cards were dispensed I was told to go and pick them up and bring them to Mistress one at a time in order. Each time I retrieved a playing card Madam put it on a table in rows according to its value and suit.

Let's make it more fun," Lady Frobisher said, I'll tell you what card I want and you go and find it. To make the game even more exciting you're to pick the card up in your mouth, if you drop it you'll get the equivalent strokes of the crop according to the value of the card, and fifteen strokes for a Joker. Let's start with the five of hearts."

I scurried around the floor looking for the five of hearts. Trying to pick up a card from the floo using my mouth only was almost an impossible task.

"No hands," Mistress warned, "Double punishment if I see you using your hands. Wher I finally got the card in my mouth and brought i to Mistress she said:

"Go on, sit up and beg like a good little doggy,' she said smiling and clearly having fun. Madan took the card from me and shook it, "Yuck, it is covered in saliva you naughty little puppy, turn around, when I did so I felt the sting of the croj on my bottom, which felt like being branded with a red hot iron. When the game was over I was covered in red welts.

"That was enjoyable," Lady Frobisher said, "Now you may dress and go and do your chore before preparing lunch.

Chapter Nine

More Secrets

Lady Frobisher had stepped up my humiliations and her little games had become an almost daily event. However, there was always time for me to do my duties which were now all household chores. One afternoon whilst I was cleaning the drawing room Madam went out to the shops locking all the doors so I couldn't leave, but it did give me a chance to open her bureau. With the aid of a paper clip, I managed to pick the crude lock and rummage through her personal documents. It was quite an Aladdin's cave I found her marriage documents, plus the death certificate for her late husband. There were also some unpaid bills. I was having quite a bit of fun leafing through her private things. Then I saw a birth certificate, which at a glance I assumed was Madam's birth certificate, but on closer inspection, I realised it was for her sister Alice who had died.

I was shocked to see not only did she share my first name but she was exactly the same age as me and shared the same birthday. I carried on hunting to see if I could find her death certificate but it was nowhere in the bureau. This worried me could I be Lady Frobisher's sister? Have I been misled all these years could I be her sibling? If that were the case, then I might be the true owner of Weeping Willow Cottage, but how do I prove such a thing? One thing is for sure I was not her sister's child as I am the same age as her sister. Had I been lied to about that as well?

I thought I heard Mistress returning so I quickly put everything back as it was and locked the bureau. I then continued with my chores as I heard Mistress in the hall taking off her hat and coat.

"There you are Alice," she said coming into the drawing room and noticing me dusting. "You can stop doing that for a moment and go and make a pot of tea, I'm parched." When I returned with a pot of tea and biscuits and placed them on the table I asked:

'Madam, may I ask what happened to your sister Alice, how did she die?" Madam looked up at me with a curious look of scorn.

'You speak only when spoken to Alice, I see I shall have to spend more time reinforcing this concept as you have trouble understanding it. Besides, why do you ask?"

'I was just curious Madam, you never talk about her," I replied.

"Well, go and take your curiosity somewhere else and do your chores, away with you," She said dismissing the subject. I left the matter there, but it did bug me and played on my mind. It was too much of a coincidence for her sister to share my first name and be the same age as me exactly. How was I to get to the bottom of the matter?

A few days later, Madam seemed to be in one of her better moods. I was busy in the bedroom brushing her hair and we were chatting away about all sorts of things when I decided to ask again about her sister Alice. If anything my question went down even worse than my last attempt at asking it. Lady Frobisher turned in an instant from being friendly and jovial to the tyrant she is best suited for.

"What business is it of yours young lady? You're the servant and should be asking such questions about your Mistress. You are forgetting your place I think we shall have to nip that in the bud or who knows where it will end. Stop brushing my hair and take your clothes off," She said standing from her seat. She went to a cupboard and got some leather cuffs and put them on my wrists. Then she attached a chain to my collar and dragged me down the stairs naked and out of the front door. I was pulled across the gravel on my bare feet until we reached a barn. I was told to open the doors and go in. The barn was completely empty apart from a few tea chests and the odd bale of straw. Madam tied some rope to my wrist cuffs and throw them over a beam and took up the slack until my arms were stretched out. Then she put what she called a leg spreader bar between my angles to stop me from closing my feet.

Lying on one of the bales of straw was a dressage whip. Madam showed it to me as she unfurled the end.

"I am going to break you in once and for all Alice. I am going to whip you until you bleed and become totally docile and complaint. See this as a lesson in knowing your place so you never ever speak out of turn again. I now want you to count the strokes and say thank you Mistress after each lash. We'll stop when you feel warm blood trickling down your back and buttocks."

Then Madam stood back and the whipping began. I turned and twisted on my ropes, but th lashes kept coming. Madam kept true to her word and she whipped and whipped until I felt the blood seep from some of the welts. Then when I thought I was about to pass out she stopped, walked to the barn door and left me alone naked tied to a beam in a cold dark barn. After a couple of hours of absence, Madam returned.

"Have you finally learnt your lesson?" she asked, lifting my chin and looking into my tear-swollen eyes. "Speak," she growled, "or do you need another whipping to reduce you to the slave I need? Beg to go down on your knees and kiss my feet. I want to hear your contrition." I begged, but my mouth was sore and dry and I could hardly form the words necessary. "Speak up my girl I want to hear you loud and clear. Then she took off the leg spreader and lowered the ropes. "Now on all fours and kiss my feet."

I dropped to my knees and went on all fours and licked and kissed Madam's feet. Lady Frobisher started to walk towards the barn door.

'Did I tell you to stop kissing my feet Alice?" she asked as she slowly walked to the barn doors and across the gravel to the house's front door. With me crawling along behind trying to kiss her feet. At the front door, she stopped and looked down at me on all fours and said:

"Have you finally learned your lesson to speak only when spoken to and to be totally obedient?" I nodded. "Now let me hear you say you want to be my docile compliant maid and I'll have no further trouble from you," I repeated what Madam had said and I was allowed into the house. "You may sleep on the scullery floor tonight I don't want you getting blood all over your sheets."

With those remarks, I was allowed to dress in ar old tattered nightgown to save blood on my uniform and told to prepare dinner. The only saving grace was the kitchen was warm and it allowed me to thaw out and warm up from hours in the freezing cold barn. Whilst cooking nursed my wounds and put cream on some of the worst welts.

Chapter Ten

The Three Wise Men

Life continued as normal. I confess I had become more docile and more compliant. Madam had succeeded in breaking me in, I couldn't bear another session in the barn or a cold night in the shed, I had had enough and it was hard enough to bare the daily insults and humiliations Madam bestowed on me. I had become the very creature she craved, except a tiny part of me still agonised over whether or not I was indeed her sister and not her niece. I accepted my fate, though, and stopped rebelling and got on with being a very lowly servant to a very demanding Mistress.

However, one afternoon Wilfred Drummer and his two brothers arrived at the cottage. I showed them into the drawing room and I could see by Madam's face she was not expecting them to call. In her usual insincere fashion, she welcomed them in and told them to sit and sent me off to make a pot of coffee. The arrival of these men had tweaked my interest and I deliberately left the drawing-room door slightly ajar so I might hear what is being said in the kitchen as I brewed the coffee.

"We have some good news for you Lady Frobisher," said Wilfred looking at his brothers for approval. Brian has studied your late husband's accounts and when we were paying off his debts and reimbursing you monies left over from settling all your husband's affairs, w

)ticed your husband has overseas properties, hich were never taken into account when osing his accounts. On closer inspection, it as discovered these properties needn't be cluded in your husband's debts because they ere registered in your sister's name we assume was a dodge to avoid tax. However, as your ster is now deceased, they become by default ur properties to do with as you wish."

Ve have come to ask if you would like us to ll these properties as we assume you have no e for them?" asked Colin enthusiastically. The le should realise a considerable amount of oney, not enough to buy back Frobisher Hall, it enough to live very comfortably for the rest 'your life,"

)h yes, please do sell them for me as soon as u can," said Lady Frobisher, who was solutely delighted with the news.

"I will just step outside to go to my coach and get some forms which I shall need you to sign," suggested Wilfred. Wilfred got up from his seat and left the room and passed me to go to the front door. I followed him outside. He opened the coach door and began to fumble through some papers in a briefcase. He saw out of the corner of his eye me approaching.

I was having second thoughts about speaking with the man when he turned and said:

"Yes young lady you seem anxious to speak with me," he observed whilst waiting for me to say something. "Come on lass spit it out," he said I don't have all day, besides, there is a bitter wind and I am anxious to get back inside the house before I freeze to death.

"Sorry," I said feebly. "I don't mean to hold yc up. Can I ask a question in confidence? I mean you won't go telling Madam, I have spoken to you."

"Yes, I am intrigued, go on, I promise whatever you say will remain between the two of us."

"It's a simple question," I said, feeling braver about speaking. Have you personally seen Madam's sister Alice Frobisher's death certificate? Are you sure she is dead and if so how did she die?"

"Why do you ask?" Wilfred inquired not understanding why I should be interested in such a matter when after all I am just the maid.

"I know this sounds daft," I replied, "but I think I might be Alice Frobisher." Wilfred laughed and told me I was being silly.

'My name is Alice and I am the same age and the same date of birth. I have always lived with Lady Frobisher, and have been her ward since I was an infant. I was told I am Madam's niece, but how can I be I'm too old to be her niece, but the right age to be Madam's sister Alice."

"Have you seen your own birth certificate?" Wilfred asked.

"Never my last name is supposed to be Simms, but is it? I have no proof of such," I replied.

"Then how do you know your date of birth?" He asked.

"Simply because that was what I was told when I was small," I replied. "All I want is proof Alice Frobisher is dead."

"I am not a solicitor only an accountant although there are solicitors in my office, I will try and source Alice Frobisher's death certificate and when I call next I will let you know what I have found. I will also try and find your birth certificate so you can be a bit more certain about who you are. Now I must get back to the drawing room or Lady Frobisher will wonder where I am," The man said going back to the house with his papers. I thanked Mr Drummer profusely and I was convinced he genuinely wanted to help me.

I had forgotten all about my verbal exchange with Wilfred Drummer as the weeks turned into months and I had seen nothing of him or his brothers. I was quite happy to forget the matter as I felt a bit childish in approaching Wilfred Drummer and that I would have just come across as a silly confused little maid worrying about things way above her station in life.

Madam of course still spent lots of time and effort making sure I understood my place in life. I suppose there were worse things than being a kivvy and a sex slave at least I could count on three meals a day and a roof, why should I strive for anything better? I was beginning to understand good girls get to share Madam's bed and bad girls get the scullery floor, that was the reality of my life.

I learned to keep my head down and just get on with my chores and I was mostly left alone until Madam wanted some sexual relief. I realised she had no interest in men at all. I had never known her to have a boyfriend or male visitors apart from her husband when he was alive and she didn't see much of him either. Madam was in my opinion a lesbian who got most of her sexual needs with me. A sexual sadist who not only got her thrills by caressing and fondling me, but she also delighted in making me suffer and inflicting pain.

My Mistress had a new toy made especially for me and kept in the bedroom. Madam described it as El Burro (A Spanish Donkey) or wooden horse, a torture device used exclusively on women during the Spanish Inquisition. The triangular device was designed sharply angled and pointing upward, mounted on horse-leg-like support poles. When disobedient I was forced to ride on the wooden horse while naked for up to two hours at a time. Madam would chain me to the horse and would adjust the wooden trestle until I was on tiptoe and then left me to my own devices, knowing I had to sit occasionally to rest my feet. When I did sit the upright frame would cut into my vagina making it very painful and sore. It was an exquisite punishment and required no interaction from Mistress.

When I was sufficiently sore I would be put on the bed and she would use a strap on, on me until I screamed for her to stop. I knew I had to do something I couldn't continue to live like this for the rest of my life. Then one afternoon Wilfred Drummer returned to the house alone. I answered the door and was eager to ask him if he had none anything about what we discussed weeks before. He said he would find time to speak to me before he left. I showed him into the drawing room where Madam, as usual, was doing her embroidery.

Madam looked excited as she put down her work and invited Wilfred to sit and sent me off for the obligatory pot of coffee.

"I presume you have called by to tell me my lat husband's properties have been sold. How muc have I made from the sales?" She asked rubbin; her hands together in expected glee.

"I am sorry to inform you Lady Frobisher, I have encountered a problem and the sale of the properties has been suspended.

"A problem," Madam barked. "What sort of problem? How do you mean suspended?"

"Before we can sell the properties the probate authorities tell us we need a copy of your late sister's death certificate. We have tried to source it ourselves, but are unable to find a copy from the births, deaths and marriage office. I presume you have the original may I see it please?" He asked.

"I don't understand nobody has ever asked for it before," Lady Frobisher said in disgust. "Is it absolutely necessary?"

"Well, we will need to see it before I can allow the properties to be sold," Wilfred said apologetically. It is insisted by the probate office and has nothing to do with me or my colleagues."

'It may take me a while to find it you'll need to call again," Madam said fuming as she stood and paced the room.

"There is also another matter I wish to discuss with you," Wilfred went on to say.

"Another matter what other matter?" Madam asked, getting hotter under the collar by the minute.

"Your maid Alice Simms, we have been looking for her birth certificate and we are unable to find that as well." The man said.

"What on earth do you want my maid's birth certificate for, she has nothing to do with the matter in hand," Lady Frobisher expounded.

"Your maid Alice has asked me to find it for her and she has never seen her birth certificate and has never had a copy." Wilfred went on to say.

"I am not paying you to sort out my maid's affairs," Lady Frobisher said indignantly.

"No Madam, you won't be charged for this service it is something I have offered to do for your maid and I wondered if you might be holding her birth certificate for her in safe keeping.

"No, no," Lady Frobisher replied, "I do not have my maid's birth certificate."

"Well, that concludes my business I will return in a couple of days to give you time to find your sister's death certificate. Once I have the documentation the properties can be sold quite quickly."

Wilfred left without touching his coffee. He whispered to me on the way out, everything was being sorted and he'll have more news for me shortly. I didn't question him I let him go about his business as I had overheard everything that had been said between him and Lady Frobisher, so I knew the matter was in hand. This had raised my spirits, but I am not so sure about Lady Frobisher, Once Wilfred had gone, she paced up and down the drawing-room floor clearly fretting about something.

I guessed it was because there was no death certificate to be found and Madam's world was about to tumble around her feet. The tables are about to be turned soon I can be the voyeur of her anguish and misfortune. Revenge is indeed sweet and a dish to be served cold. All I had to do is abide by my time and wait for Madam's house of cards to slip and crumble. If I turned out to be Lady Frobisher's sister Weeping Willow Cottage will be mine an exquisite thought I would savour until the return of Wilfred Drummer.

Chapter Eleven

Madam's slips from virtue

As promised Wilfred Drummer returned to Weeping Willow Cottage anticipating the handover of Lady Frobisher's sister's death certificate.

"I am so sorry, Mr Drummer," Lady Frobisher said apologetically. "I haven't been able to track down my sister's death certificate. "Would a letter from me certified by a notary be enough to satisfy the probate authorities?"

I am sorry, Madam, it would not. Only a death certificate will suffice. I have also sent Brian Drummer to Somerset House, where all the birth, death and marriage documents are kept to crawl through their files to find your maid's birth certificate as it may have a bearing on the matter in hand as we believe she may be your sister and is very much alive."

"Poppycock," Lady Frobisher said with an insincere and very animated laugh. "What absurd nonsense, this is not what I pay you for."

"We'll see, anyway I must go now, we'll be in touch very shortly," Wilfred said leaving the room. I was coming in with a pot of coffee as he was about to leave and he smiled and gave me a wink as he passed, to say everything was in hand. Unfortunately, he had done nothing to improve Madam's mood.

"You have split the coffee, you foolish woman, Lady Frobisher barked. I am sure she split it herself so she could have a go at me. "Your standards are slipping badly I shall have to punish you. Madam went to a drawer and retrieved a long leather riding crop and some soft rope. "Hold out your hand at your side palm up," she said pulling me into the centre of the room. I was made to keep my hand up until I received six of the crop, and then she set to work on my other hand which also got six strokes. I was already in tears when she demanded:

"Clear the table," while she waited for me to clear everything off with my swollen hands she profusely bent and flicked the crop. When the table was cleared I was bent across it and she tied my hands to the legs at the far side. Then she tied my legs to the table legs on the other side until I was unable to move a muscle.

"So you think you're my sister, do you? We'll see about that. You have delusions of grandeur my girl, we'll soon bring you back down to earth you little useless, good-for-nothing wrench." Then she waded into me with the whip, the whipping seemed to last forever until my bottom looked like tenderised meat. Then I was untied and dragged into the scullery and made to go on my knees. I had a bucket and scrubbing brush thrown at me. I filled the bucket with warm water and poured in some detergent.

"Now on the floor on your knees and get scrubbing. I'll be here to watch and give encouragement," she said striking my already sore bottom with her crop. I started to scrub. Madam pointed out places where I missed and I had to crawl back and scrub that area again.

"This is where you belong, Alice, on the floor scrubbing for your Mistress this is your calling. You're my slave, that is all you are, all you will ever be just my skivvy. You have missed another bit there," she said, pointing with the end of her whip. "Lick it," she screamed. "I want to see you licking the floor, go on do as you're told, you useless little worthless wrench,' Madam was getting very animated and I though she might burst a vessel or have a heart attack. I started to lick, but my eyes were filling with tears and I couldn't see properly. Just as I was about to be whipped again the doorbell rang. Madam stopped in her tracks and looked towards the front door.

"Who could that be?" she asked under her breath. I can't send you to the door, you're soaking wet, stay here until I get back," she barked to me as she left for the front door. I crawled over to where I could see Madam open the front door.

Stood before her, were two strangers in dark coats and a uniformed constable. A tall man wearing a trilby hat asked:

"Are you Lady Jane Frobisher?"

"Yes," replied Madam faltering, sensing something bad was about to befall her.

"I have a warrant for your immediate arrest," he said apologetically. "I am afraid you'll need to come with me to Saint Thomas Police Station."

"A warrant for my arrest, don't be so absurd what for?" Madam repeated, feeling giddy at the knees.

"I am sorry to say, Madam, you're suspected of fraud and you'll have to come with me now," The man said beckoning her towards a waiting carriage.

" Okay, if I must, I'll just get my coat and have a quick word with my maid," she insisted. The constable nodded that was okay and she got her fir coat from the hall and came over to me.

"There has been a bit of a misunderstanding," Lady Frobisher said, looking down at me on the floor, "and I have to go to the police station. I'll be back later today," she added looking pale and quite shaken.

Chapter Twelve

What goes around comes around.

Madam didn't return until much later that day, in fact, the next person I would see is Wilfred Drummer. I answered the door and told him my Mistress was indisposed. He replied he knew, and that it was me he wished to speak to.

"Come in, come in," I said enthusiastically. "Can I offer you a cup of tea or coffee?"

"I can see you're brewing, a cup of tea will do nicely," he said, pulling a chair out from under the kitchen table.

"Will we be more comfortable in the drawing room? I asked.

"No, no, this is adequate," Wilfred replied. "I wanted to speak to you to say I did take what you had asked of me quite seriously and after a long investigation and many visits to central London, that the conclusion we have come to is you're indeed Lady Frobisher's sister."

"I knew as much," I said, bouncing up and down in excitement. "I just knew something wasn't right and I came to the conclusion no way could I be her niece I am too old."

"Do you know why Lady Frobisher was arreste by the police?" the man asked as he sipped his cup of tea.

"Only that she is accused of fraud," I replied, unsure of myself and only going on what I hear at the door when the police visited.

"That's right, she has been arrested for fraud. This is because Weeping Willow Cottage, overseas properties, most of Lady Frobisher's pension allowance etcetera, all belong to you. It is a lot to think about so I won't tax you with all this right now, but later, perhaps we can discuss managing your affairs"

"Oh yes, it's a lot to absorb. What will happen to Lady Frobisher?" I asked.

"I expect the police will release her on bail sometime today. She may go to prison, but that is down to the courts, more likely she'll get probation. She'll need to return here to collect her clothes and things, it depends on how generous you are whether or not she can stay for a few days until she finds alternative accommodation."

Wilfred got up to leave. I showed him to the front door, but before he left he asked:

'The change in Lady Frobisher's fortunes will be quite a shock for her, so I trust you'll show compassion in your dealings with her." With those words, he left for his carriage.

"Compassion," I mused to myself. "I'll show Lady Frobisher compassion when I see her next."

I didn't have too long to wait for at around 5 pm a coach pulled up outside the cottage and I saw the tall, thin outline of Lady Frobisher alight from the carriage and walk towards the door.

I went to the door to open it so she could pass and then I thought. "What am I doing, she can knock." So I waited there, on the other side of the door waiting for her to knock. Finally, she did so and I opened the door to see a very contrite and humiliated Lady Frobisher. The lady also looked tired and pale as she entered the hallway. I could see she has had a harrowing time at the police station.

"I'll put the kettle on," I said, kicking myself for being so thoughtful. I felt sorry for her, but only fleetingly. Madam left her coat in the hall and came into the kitchen and sat on the same seat as Wilfred was using an hour or two earlier.

"I suppose you have heard by now," the woman said looking at me fearfully.

"Yes," I said, pouring her a tea. "Wilfred Drummer called by earlier and told me the news that I am actually your sister and not your niece."

"Did he say anything else?" Madam asked.

"Yes, quite a bit actually, he told me everything you own including this house is actually mine."

"When do you want me to leave?" Lady Frobisher asked and added, "you realise if I leave here I only have one place I can go."

"The workhouse," I said, answering for her barely hiding my delight. I felt a surge of anger and emotion welling up inside of me. "Would you like me to call you a carriage to take you to the poorhouse, it is the least I can do considering."

"Don't be too harsh with me, I have looked after you all these years."

"Look after me, look after me," I repeated incredulously. "Using a whip on me is looking after me, is it? Do you think I have forgotten the night I slept in the shed, or being tied to a Spanish Donkey and whipped in the barn?"

"Get your things and I'll go and hail you a carriage. I will stand at the door and wave you off that is how compassionate I feel."

Lady Frobisher went upstairs to pack a bag, in the meantime, I tried to calm my emotions which were bubbling over. I decided as I waited or her to pack, sending Madam to the poorhouse wasn't punishment enough and I wouldn't be there to see her distress and enjoy her discomforts. I wanted to wallow and immerse myself in her change of circumstances. So whilst Madam was busy packing I went upstairs myself to fetch something.

I returned to the kitchen before her and waited for my former Mistress to come downstairs. Madam slowly and contritely walked into the kitchen and put her bag down.

"May I wait here until my carriage arrives?" she asked.

"I'll pour you another cup of tea whilst we wait," I said without emotion. I poured her a cup and sat myself down with a cup. I watched her for a moment or two without speaking. I could sense her anguish and discomfort.

"On reflection, I have a proposition for you," I said after some thought. "I am a fool to myself, should by all rights let you rot in a workhouse for what you have done to me. Nevertheless, I have something for you to consider."

"Yes," Lady Frobisher said, "yes, please let me hear it, anything but let me go to the poorhouse." I pointed to a chair between us. Lady Frobisher looked at the chair and noticed a garment hanging over the back.

"It's your maid's uniform," Lady Frobisher said not quite understanding.

"Yes, it will fit you until we can find something better," I replied.

"You want me to be your maid," Madam asked disbelieving the stark choice in front of her.

"I promise to treat you no worse than you did me. The choice is yours, you can go upstairs ar put on the uniform or you can take your bag and go and stand on the pavement until your coach arrives. So which will it be the dress or the workhouse?"

Madam with tears in her eyes, without saying a further word, picked up the uniform and went back upstairs to get changed.

The End

Check out my other books:

The Chronicles of a Male Slave.

A real-life account of a consensual slave. The book follows the life of an individual who comes to terms with his submissive side and his search for a Mistress and his subsequent experiences as a consensual slave.

This book gives a real insight into the B.D.S.M.,

lifestyle and what it is like to be a real slave to a lifestyle Mistress.

Mistress Margaret.

This is the story of young teenage Brenden, who is finding out about his sexuality when he meets older Mistress Margaret a nonprofessional dominatrix. Mistress Margaret takes Brenden's hand and shows him the mysterious, erotic world of BDSM and all it has to offer.

The Week That Changed My Life.

A tale about a young girl discovering her sexuality with an older, more mature dominant man whilst on a week's holiday by the sea. She was introduced into a world of BDSM that would change her outlook on life forever.

The Temple of Gor.

Hidden in the wilds of Scotland is The Temple of Gor, a secret BDSM society. In the Temple, you will find Masters and their female slaves living in a shared commune. The community is based on the Gorean subculture depicted in a fictional novel by John Norman and has taken a step too far and turned into a macabre reality. Stella a young girl from England, stumbles on the commune and is captured and turned into a Kajira slave girl until she finds a way to escape her captors.

Becoming a Sissy Maid.

This is a true story of one person's quest to become a sissy maid for a dominant couple. The story outlines the correspondence between the Master, Mistress, and sissy maid, which leads up to their first and second real-time meeting.

It is a fascinating tale and is a true, honest and accurate account, only the names and places have been changed to protect the individuals involved. It is a must-be-read book by anyone into BDSM and will give an interesting insight for anyone wishing to become in the future a real-time sissy maid.

Meet Maisy The Sissy Maid.

This story is about Maisy a sissy maid and her life. The story takes Maisy through all the various stages a sissy has to make take to find her true submissive and feminine self. It is a long and arduous road and many transitions before Maisy finds true happiness as a lady's maid for her Mistress.

Beginner's Guide For The Serious Sissy

So you want to be a woman and dress and behave like a sissy? You accept you cannot compete with most men and now want to try something new and different. This guide will help you along the way and walk the potential sissy through the advantages and pitfalls of living as a submissive woman.

Becoming a serious sissy requires making changes that are both physical and mental. This will involve learning to cross-dress, leg-crossing, sit, stand, bend hair removal, wear makeup, use cosmetics, and sit down to pee.

You'll learn feminine mannerisms such as stepping daintily, arching your spine, swishing your hips, and adopting a feminine voice. You'll understand more about hormone treatment and herbal supplements.

There is advice and tips on going out in public for the first time and coming out of the closet to friends, colleagues, and family. The guide will give help you to slowly lose your masculine identity and replace it with a softer gentle feminine one.

A Collaring For A Sissy.

Collaring ceremonies are taken very seriously by the BDSM community and are tantamount to a traditional wedding. Lots of thought and planning go into such an event and can take many forms.

Mistress Anastasia's sissy maid Paula has just completed her six months probation and has earned her collar. This is a story about Paula's service and her subsequent collaring ceremony.

The Secret Society.

Rene Glock is a freelance journalist looking for a national scoop and attempts to uncover and expose a Secret Society of Goreans which have set up residence in an old nightclub. However, as he delves into the secret world he finds he has an interest in BDSM and questions his moral right to interfere in what goes on in the Gorean Lodge.

The Good Master and Mistress Guide.

If you want to become a good Dominant and practice BDSM in a safe and considerate way, then this guide is for you.

It is written by a submissive that has had many dominants male and female over the years and knows what goes into becoming a good dominant and the mistakes some dominants make.

The book is not aimed to teach, but to make the fledgling dominant understand what is going on in the dominant-submissive dynamic, so they can understand their charges better and become better dominants.

My Transgender Journey

This is a true story with some minor alterations to protect people's identities. It is a tale about my own journey into transgender and my eventual decision to come out.

It is hoped that others can share my experiences, relate to them and perhaps take comfort from some of them.

The book has some BDSM content but is only used to put my story into context, it's about my experiences, trials and tribulations of coming out and living as a female full-time.

I hope you enjoy my little story.

Cinders

Cinders is the BDSM version of Cinderella. It is a story where an orphaned Tommy is sent to be brought up by his aunt and two very beautiful sisters.

The sisters were cruel and taunting and dressed Tommy up like a Barbie Doll. One day Tommy was caught with auntie's bra and knickers and as a punishment, he was a feminist and turned into Nancy the maid. Poor Nancy is consigned to a life of drudgery and final acceptance of life as a menial skivvy.

This story doesn't have a glass slipper or a prince, but Nancy is given a present of some new rubber gloves and a bottle of bleach. There is no happy ending or is there, you decide.

At The Races

Ryan is a hotel night porter and is at a crossroads in his life. He feels his talents are being wasted in a job with no future. Through a friend, he is offered a managerial position on a farm in Catalonia, Spain. He decides to take the post but has no idea what sort of farm he is going to work at.

Only on the flight out to Spain does Ryan realise that there is more to the farm than rearing chickens and growing vegetables. Later he learns the main event of the year is The Derby and there isn't a horse in sight.

I Nearly Married A Dominatrix

This is a true story that I have changed a little bit to protect people from identification. It's a story about a man's constant struggle and fights against his deep-rooted need to be submissive and a woman who conversely, is very comfortable with her dominance and heavily into the BDSM lifestyle.

They meet and get along very well indeed until Mistress Fiona announces she wants to become a professional dominatrix. Rex, the submissive boyfriend goes along with his Mistress's plans, reluctantly, but as time goes by there are more and more complications heaped on the relationship until it snaps.

Be careful what you ask for

There is an old English adage: Be careful about what you ask for; it may come true.

This is a story about a BDSM fantasy that has gone badly wrong.

Fantasy is simply a fantasy and we all have them regardless of our sexuality. Fantasies are quite harmless until we choose to act them out for real and when do act out our fantasies the line between fantasy and reality can become very blurred. This is a tale about one person's fantasy that becomes all too real for comfort.

Petticoat Lane.

A slightly effeminate young boy is taken under the wings of his school teacher. She becomes his guardian and trains him to become a servant girl to serve her for the rest of his life.

An unexpected incident happens and Lucy the maid has an opportunity to escape her life of drudgery and servitude, but does she take the opportunity or does she stay with her Mistress?

The Life and Times of a Victorian Maid.

This is a story about the life and times of a young Transgender who becomes a Victorian-style maid in a large exclusively B.D.S.M. household. Although fiction this story is largely based on fact, as the author herself lived in such a household for a while as a maid.

It shows the contrast between a place of safety where like-minded people can live in relative harmony and the need for ridged discipline in it serving staff.

There are many thriving households, such as th one mentioned here, tucked away out of sight and away from prying minds.

I Became a Kajira slave girl.

A Gorean scout Simon, who is looking for new talent kidnaps Emma a PhD student on sabbatical with her friend Zoey in Spain. Emma is half-drugged and sent across the ocean to the United States and ends up in the clandestine City of Gor in the Mojave desert sixty miles from civilization.

Here there is no law women are mere objects for the pleasure of men. Emma becomes a Kajira a female slave whose sole purpose in life is to please her master or be beaten tortured or killed.

Two years into Emma's servitude and she meets Simon again. Simon is consumed with guilt when he sees what Emma has been reduced to, a beaten, downtrodden and abused slave. He vows to free her from her servitude, But how they are in one of the biggest deserts in the world and sixty miles from anywhere?

Training My First Sissy Maid.

A young single mother with a part-time job, two teenage children, and up to her knees in housework is at the end of her tether and finding it harder and harder to cope.

Then reading one of her daughter's kinky magazines she found in her bedroom whilst tidying, read an article about sissy maids who are willing to work without pay just for discipline, control and structure to their lives. Excited about the prospect she decides a maid is an answer to her domestic problems.

She sets about finding a sissy to come and do her housework and be trained and moulded into becoming her loyal obedient sissy maid. On the journey she discovers she is a natural dominant and training her maid becomes a highly erotic and fulfilling experience.

A Week with Mistress Sadistic.

Susan a young female reporter in her thirties wants to know more about B.D.S.M for a future article in her magazine. She arranged to spend a week with Mistress Sadistic and watch how a professional dominatrix works.

After an eye-opening week of watching Mistress Sadistic deal with her many and varied clients, Mistress Sadistic wonders if Susan might be submissive and puts her to the text to make Susan her personal slave.

Lady Frobisher and her maid Alice.

This is a gripping tale of BDSM in Victorian England. It is a story about the lives of Lady Frobisher and her hapless maid Alice. It is a tale of lesbianism and sexual sadism with a twist at the end.

If you enjoy reading BDSM literature you'll love this as it has everything woven into an interesting tale of two people's lives at the top end of society.

K9

This is a tale that explores an area of B.D.S.M where a Mistress or Master desires a human dog (submissive) to train and treat as a real dog in every respect. Mistress Cruella is one such Mistress who takes on a young male submissive as her human dog and she takes the role of Mistress and her dog very seriously indeed.

Ryan soon becomes Max the Poodle and he struggles with his new role as a pooch but learns to be an obedient dog to please his Mistress. Max soon discovers there is far more to being a dog than meets the eye.

Bridget Monroe's Finishing School for Sissies.

Bridget and her husband are both dominant and have their own sissy maid Isabel to help them with housework. One day when the couple were on holiday in Kent, Bridget discovered an empty manor house in need of extensive repairs. On inquires, she decides to buy the manor but soon realises that to pay for the mortgage and repair costs the manor house will need to be run as a business.

Bridget used willing slaves in the B.D.S.M., community to help repair and renovate the manor house and later it was decided on advice from friends to open the manor house as a finishing school for sissies. A business had been born and later other B.D.S.M., activities were added to the core business, which included torture rooms and a medieval dungeon. Once a month an open day was held at the academy held pony races, yard sales and schoolboy classes. This also included K9 dog shows, beer tents and other amenities intending to satisfy the whole B.D.S.M., community.

Just when the business was taking off and in profit disaster struck. Society wasn't ready for Bridget Monroe's Finishing School for Sissies and Bridget was forced to close.

Printed in Great Britain
by Amazon

37952633R00089